Everyone has a favourite character in The Wind
in the Willows.
The practical yet poetic Rat, the sentimental,
lovable Mole, or even the bombastic Toad.
The youngest readers will love the book just
for the splendid story but older ones will enjoy
the atmosphere of the river, the Wild Wood,
the cosy homes of the little animals and the
magnificence of Toad Hall and Badger's vast
underground tunnels.
There is excitement and laughter in the
remarkable adventures of Toad, who is quite
sure that he can outwit everybody and gets into
a great deal of trouble while trying to do so.
Ratty's love of the river, Toad's enthusiasm for
everything that is new and Mole's acceptance of
any good idea, give each animal a character of
his own, backed up by Badger's down to earth
reasoning and help when danger threatens.

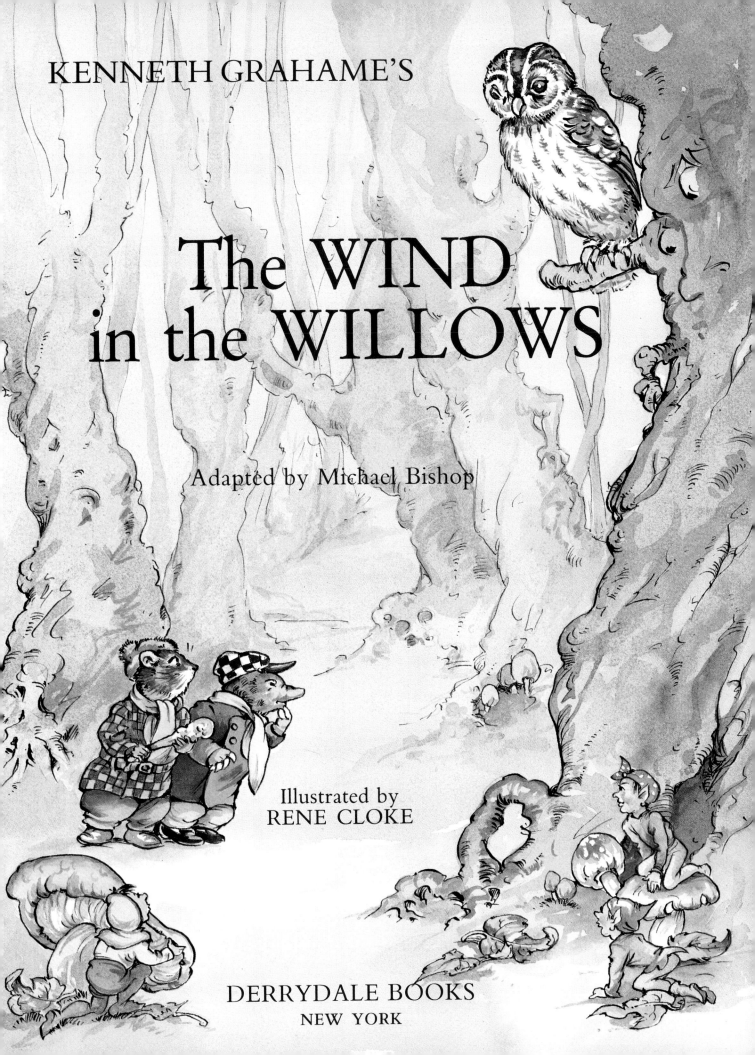

KENNETH GRAHAME'S

# The WIND in the WILLOWS

Adapted by Michael Bishop

Illustrated by
RENE CLOKE

DERRYDALE BOOKS

NEW YORK

ISBN 0 517 492849

Text Copyright © 1985 Award Publications Limited
Illustrations Copyright © 1985 Award Publications Limited
This edition first published in USA 1985 by Derrydale Books,
a division of Crown Publishers, Inc.
225 Park Avenue South New York, New York 10003
Printed in Belgium

c d e f g h

# CONTENTS

## Chapter 1

## THE RIVER BANK

Mole had been working very hard all morning, spring-cleaning.

First with brooms and dusters, then standing on a little table with a brush and a pot of paint, slap-slap, up-and-down, till he was aching all over.

Suddenly he flung down his brush, said "Bother!" and "Hang spring-cleaning!", and bolted out of the house into the fields outside.

"This is fine," he said to himself. "This is better than painting the house!"

First he met some rabbits as he rambled along the hedgerows.

Soon he found himself by a river. Mole sat down on the grassy bank and then he saw – coming out of a dark hole on the other side – a brown little face with whiskers.

It was the Water Rat.

"Hullo, Mole," said Rat, "I'll come over in my boat to fetch you."

"Do you know, I've never been in a boat before in all my life," said Mole.

"What!" cried Rat. "In that case, let's go down the river together and make a day of it!"

He rowed quickly back across the water with Mole. Rat popped into his hole in the bank and came staggering out a few moments later with a heavy picnic basket.

They rowed down the
river, past the Wild Wood,
as far as an old water mill.

There, Rat brought his boat
alongside the river bank, so that they
could set out the picnic.

"What have we got?" asked
Mole, who was hungry.

"There's chicken and ham
and salad and lemonade and
cake and chocolate
biscuits…"

"Oh, my!" said Mole.

A few minutes later, when they were feeling *much* better and not so hungry, a very wet and furry head suddenly appeared out of the water above the edge of the river bank.

It was Otter.

"You greedy beggars!" he said. "Why didn't you invite me?"

And he set about helping them finish up the picnic.

"All the world seems to be out on the river today," said Otter, wiping his paws on his whiskers.

"Toad's out for one, in his brand new boat, and wearing his new boating clothes."

Just then, Toad flashed into view, rowing rapidly past the water mill. Rat stood up excitedly and waved to him, but Toad just shook his head and rowed on.

By now they had eaten all the food.

Otter was in the middle of telling them a story
about Toad – and beginning to feel a bit peckish again
– when suddenly he saw a juicy mayfly.

With hardly a splash, he was gone.

So Mole and Rat packed up the picnic things and
got back into the boat to go home.

Rat was rowing gently along when Mole said, "Ratty, please, *I* want to row now."

"Not yet, Mole," replied Rat. "It's not as easy as it looks."

But Mole jumped up and grabbed the oars, knocking Rat backwards.

"Stop it!" cried Rat. "You'll have us both over!"

And over they went – SPLOOSH – and they were both struggling in the water.

Rat, of course, was a good swimmer and thought it was very funny.

Having rescued Mole and got him to the river bank to dry off, he plunged back into the water to recover his boat.

Finally, he dived down to the bottom of the river to rescue the picnic basket.

"I *am* sorry, Ratty," said Mole dejectedly.

When they eventually got back home, Rat sat Mole in front of a bright fire to warm him up.

And to cheer him up, he told him river stories until supper-time.

So supper was a very happy meal. And soon afterwards Rat showed a very sleepy Mole upstairs to the best bedroom for the night.

## Chapter 2

# THE OPEN ROAD

**R**at was sitting on the river bank one bright summer morning, singing a song, when Mole said, "Please, Ratty, would you take me to call on Mr. Toad?"

"Why, certainly," said the good-natured Rat. "We'll go in the boat."

"There's Toad Hall," said Rat as they rounded a bend in the river. "Toad is rather rich, you know. Come along and let's find him."

Toad saw them coming across the lawn.

"Hooray!" he cried. "This is splendid. You are the very animals I wanted to see! You've got to help me."

"Is it about rowing?" asked Rat.

"Oh – I've given that up long ago," said Toad airily. "No – I've discovered the real thing. Come with me just as far as the stable yard and you shall see!"

And there it was – a gipsy caravan, shining and new, painted yellow and green with red wheels.

"Who's for a life on the open road – here today, up and off somewhere else tomorrow," said Toad gaily.

"This is the finest cart of its sort that was ever built. Come inside and have a look – planned it all myself!"

Mole was tremendously interested inside, but Rat just sat on the doorstep.

"All complete," said Toad. "Chocolate biscuits, tinned fruit, lemonade – even games to play! You'll find that nothing has been forgotten when we make our start this afternoon."

"Did I hear," said Rat slowly, "something about 'we' and 'start this afternoon'?"

"Oh, come on, Ratty, I want to show you the world!" said Toad.

There was quite an argument, but in the end Toad was able to persuade Mole and Rat to go with him.

And so, they harnessed Toad's horse and set off through the lovely countryside.

Friendly passers-by called out "Good day!" to them, or stopped to say nice things about their beautiful caravan.

And lots of rabbits sat up on their hind legs and said "Oh, my! Oh, my!" as they saw them pass by.

Late in the evening, tired and happy and miles from home, they stopped and had supper, sitting on the grass by the roadside.

Toad boasted about all the things he was going to do.

He talked until he was too tired to go on and they all went to bed in their little bunks in the caravan.

Poor Rat was obviously missing the river.

"Shall we run away tomorrow?" whispered Mole.

"No," whispered back Rat. "We'll stick by Toad until this trip is ended. He wouldn't be safe by himself!"

Nor was he safe with Mole and Rat!

Next day, as they were going along the road – Mole leading the horse, and Toad and Rat walking behind the caravan – there was suddenly an imperious "Poop-poop" behind them.

A motor car whizzed by in a cloud of dust and noise. The horse bucked and reared, dragging poor Mole off his feet.

The caravan finished up in the ditch. And Toad finished up sitting in the middle of the road.

It was a long walk for the three animals to the nearest town, where they found somebody to look after the horse and what was left of the caravan.

But Toad wasn't at all upset. He could talk of nothing but that wonderful thing, the motor car, which had caused the accident.

Next evening, when Mole was sitting by the river, fishing, Rat came up. "Heard the news?" he said. "Toad has ordered a large and expensive motor car!"

Chapter 3

# THE WILD WOOD

For a long time, Mole had wanted to meet the Badger, but Rat obviously was not keen.

So one day at the beginning of winter, while Rat dozed in front of his fire, Mole set off to explore the Wild Wood, hoping to bump into Mr. Badger.

It was a cold afternoon.

Everything was very still.

It was getting dark.

Then the faces began....

He thought he saw a little evil wedge-shaped face looking out at him from a hole.

When he turned the thing had vanished.

Then there were faces in all the little holes, in the trees, all around.

Then the whistling began and everything seemed to be closing in on him.

As he stood still to listen anxiously, he saw something moving…

He saw a rabbit running through the trees.

Mole expected it to slow down. Instead it almost brushed him as it dashed past, muttering, "Get out of this, you fool, get out!"

And it disappeared down a friendly burrow.

Mole was very frightened and he hid under some dead leaves in a hollow.

Meanwhile, Rat had been having a lovely warm doze by the fire. When he woke up at last, he called "Moly!" several times.

But there was no answer.

Then he found that Mole's cap was missing from the peg in the hall.

And when he opened the door, he saw Mole's tracks in the mud leading away from the house – straight towards the Wild Wood.

Rat armed himself with a pair of pistols and a stout cudgel, and set off bravely into the Wild Wood.

He searched for over an hour, calling "Moly, Moly, where are you?"

At last he heard an answering little cry coming from a hole at the foot of a tree. He looked inside – and there was Mole.

"Oh Ratty," he cried, "I've been so frightened."

"Now then," said Rat, "we must pull ourselves together and get going. It would never do to spend the night here!"

"Dear Ratty," said Mole, "I'm so tired – I must rest a bit longer."

And Mole snuggled down into the dry leaves and went to sleep.

When at last Mole woke up, Rat looked outside to see if it was safe to go.

It was snowing hard and the whole Wild Wood was white.

"We must make a start and take our chance," said Rat.

They trudged for more than an hour through the snow, getting more and more lost – when Mole tripped and hurt his leg.

"Poor old Mole," said Rat. "You've cut your leg. I'll tie it up for you."

Rat was scratching away at the snow where Mole had tripped up. He found a door-scraper and was very excited.

"Some careless person has left his door-scraper lying about where it's sure to trip *everybody* up," said Mole. And he sat on it to rest his leg.

But Rat was scrabbling away again, making the snow fly in all directions – until he found a doormat.

"There!" he cried in triumph.

Poor old Mole didn't quite know what he was on about.

Rat now attacked a snow bank beside them. Mole scraped busily too.

Ten minutes hard work and they found a solid little door, painted dark green. Beside it was a brass plate, which read: MR. BADGER.

Mole was chattering away in his excitement, but Rat said, "Get up and hang on to that bell-pull, and ring as hard as you can while I hammer on the door."

# Chapter 4

# MR. BADGER

**A**t last they heard the sound of slow, shuffling footsteps approaching the door from the inside.

There was a noise of a bolt being shot back, the door opened, and there was Mr. Badger.

"Oh Badger, let us in, please!" cried Rat. "We've lost our way in the snow."

"Come on into the kitchen," said Badger kindly. "There's a fire there and supper."

Badger sat the two of them down by the fireside and told them to take off their wet coats and boots.

Then he fetched them dressing gowns and slippers and put some sticking plaster on the cut on Mole's leg.

And, as he started laying the table for a lovely supper, both Rat and Mole felt they were miles away from the Wild Wood outside.

After supper they all sat round the fire and talked about Toad's troubles with his new love of driving fast cars – until it was time for bed.

Then Mr. Badger took Rat and Mole up to the spare bedroom in the loft where there were two beds surrounded by all his winter stores.

When they came down to breakfast, very late next morning, Rat and Mole found two young hedgehogs eating porridge out of wooden bowls. They also had been lost in the snow.

And hardly had they all sat down together when there was a clanging of the doorbell, a stamping of feet in the hall, and in rushed Otter.

"They've all been so worried about you on the river bank," he cried.

Soon after breakfast, Mr. Badger sent the two hedgehogs off home and suggested the others should stay to lunch.

Mole told him how much he liked living underground.

"When lunch is over," agreed Mr. Badger, "I'll take you all round this place of mine."

And, true to his promise, he lit a lantern and showed Mole all over his house, through narrow passages, long corridors, vaults and storerooms.

When they got back to the
kitchen again, they found
that Rat was very restless.

"Come on, Mole," he said
anxiously. "We must get off
– we don't want another
night in the Wild Wood."

"It'll be all right,"
said Otter. "I'm coming
with you!"

So they all said goodbye
to Mr. Badger and Otter led
them safely home.

## Chapter 5

# DULCE DOMUM
# (HOME SWEET HOME)

One day, Rat and Mole were returning home after a long day out with Otter, when their path took them through a village.

Mole was a bit anxious, but Rat re-assured him:

"Never mind, they're all safe indoors by this time, sitting round the fire, men, women and children, dogs and cats and all."

And they slipped past unnoticed.

Once beyond the village, Rat was leading the way, so he did not notice when Mole stopped in his tracks and sniffed the air.

It was one of those mysterious fairy calls that suddenly reached him and made him tingle all over.

He sniffed again – and memories came flooding back.

Home!

Mole had scarcely given a thought to his old home since he'd left it. Now he was filled with old memories.

"Ratty!" he called, "Hold on! Come back quickly."

"Oh, come along, Mole," replied Rat cheerfully, still plodding on.

"Please stop, Ratty," pleaded poor Mole.

Mole caught up with Rat, but he was obviously so upset that Rat sat him down on a tree trunk.

"What is it, old fellow?" he asked.

Poor Mole was sobbing so hard, he could scarcely speak.

"Oh, dear! Oh, dear!" he choked. "We might have just gone back and had one look at it, Ratty.... I – I was smelling it… but you wouldn't turn back."

Rat took Mole by the paw and set off back the way they had come.

"It's no good!" cried Mole. "It's too late and it's too dark and – and think of River Bank and – and your supper!"

"Hang River Bank, and supper too!" said Rat heartily. "I'm going to find your place now, if I stay out all night. So cheer up, old chap, we'll soon be back there again."

They didn't have far to go.

Mole suddenly dived down a tunnel, to which his faithful nose had led him.

Rat followed.

It seemed a long way down, until at last Mole struck a match and lit a lantern that had been hanging on the wall.

And there it was – the little front door of his house.

Mole's face beamed at the sight of all these things so dear to him, and he hurried Rat through the door.

It was cold and damp and
musty and cheerless in the
long-neglected house. But
Rat quickly busied himself.
"The first thing we want
is a jolly good fire," he said.

And Mole, encouraged by
Rat's cheerfulness, started
dusting and polishing. Even
so, he had another fit of
the blues.
"How about your supper
Ratty?" he moaned. "I've
nothing to give you."

"Pull yourself together Mole and come with me and forage," said Rat.

They went and they looked in all the cupboards.

The result was not so very depressing after all – a tin of sardines, a box of biscuits, a German sausage and some bottles of beer.

They had just got busy with the sardine tin opener when sounds were heard from outside.

Sounds like the scuffling
of small feet in the gravel and
tiny voices....

"I think it must be the field mice," said Mole
proudly. "They go round carol singing at this time of
the year. They come to Mole End last of all; and I used
to give them hot drinks and supper too sometimes…"

"Let's have a look at them," cried Rat, jumping up
and running to the door.

It was a pretty sight.

As the door opened, one of the older field mice carrying a lantern, said: "Now then, one, two, three!"

And their shrill little voices rose on the air, singing an old-time carol.

"Well sung boys!" cried Rat when they had finished. "Come on in, all of you!"

"Oh, Ratty," cried Mole in despair. "What are we doing? We've nothing to offer them!"

"Leave all that to me," said Rat. "Here, you with the lantern," he called to one of the field mice. "Come over this way. I want to talk to you."

Rat gave him a basket and some money and sent him off to the shops with strict instructions as to what he should buy.

The rest of the field mice perched in a row on the settee.

Rat, meanwhile, was opening bottles of the beer they had found to make mulled ale.

And soon every field mouse was sipping a hot drink and forgetting he had ever been cold in his life.

"They act plays too," Mole explained to Rat.

"Hey, you!" cried Mole to one of them. "Get up and recite a bit – you were in the last play."

The field mouse got up, giggled shyly, looked around the room and remained absolutely tongue-tied.

Then the field mouse who had gone to the shops came back.

There was no more talk of recitations once the contents of the basket had been emptied on to the table. And they all ate a lovely supper.

They clattered off at last, with pockets stuffed full of goodies for small brothers and sisters at home.

When the door had closed on the last of them, Mole and Rat went back to the fireside.

They brewed themselves a last nightcap of mulled ale. Finally, Rat gave a tremendous yawn and said, "Mole, old chap, I'm ready to drop!"

"Is that your bunk? Very well, I'll take this one," said Rat. "What a splendid little house this is!"

He clambered into his bunk and went to sleep at once.

Mole was also glad to get to bed and he lay down with great joy and contentment. After all the excitements of his new life, it was good to think that he had his own home to come back to.

## Chapter 6

# MR. TOAD

On a bright, sunny morning early in the summer, Mole and Rat had been busy with the boat.

They had been painting and varnishing and mending the paddles; and they were just finishing their breakfast in the parlour when there was a heavy knock on the door.

"Bother!" said Rat, all over egg. "See who it is, Mole, will you?"

It was Mr. Badger.

He strode heavily into the room, looking very, very serious.

"Toad's hour has come," he said solemnly. "This very morning another new and very powerful motor car will arrive at Toad Hall. You two must come with me at once and stop him doing any further harm."

"Right you are!" cried Rat, starting up. "We'll rescue Toad. We'll convert him!"

The three of them set off up the road, and when they reached the carriage drive of Toad Hall, they found a shiny, new, bright red motor car standing in front of the house.

And, just as they arrived, Toad came out dressed in goggles, cap and enormous overcoat.

"Hullo, you fellows," he began cheerfully, "you're just in time to come for a jolly…"

But Rat and Mole grabbed him.

Mr. Badger strode up the steps to the front door. "Take him inside," he said sternly to his companions.

Then he turned to the chauffeur in charge of the new car.

"I'm afraid you won't be wanted today," he said. "Mr. Toad has changed his mind."

And he followed the others inside.

"Now then," said
Mr. Badger to Mole
and Rat.
"Take those silly driving
clothes off him!"

Toad was kicking and struggling, so Rat sat on him
while Mole got the motoring clothes off him bit
by bit.

"You've taken no notice of our warnings," said
Mr. Badger severely. "You're getting us all a bad
name by your furious driving."

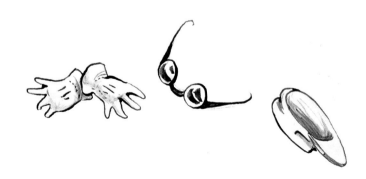

"I'll make one more effort to bring you to reason," went on Mr. Badger. "You come with me into the smoking-room."

Three-quarters of an hour later, Mr. Badger re-appeared with a limp and tearful Toad.

"He's very sorry and he's going to give up motor cars for ever," announced Mr. Badger.

Mr. Badger asked Toad to repeat in front of his
friends what he had just said in the smoking-room.

They all looked at him.

"No!" he said. "I'm not sorry. In fact the first motor
car I see, 'poop–poop!' Off I go in it!"

"What," cried Mr. Badger. "You backsliding
animal you… Take him upstairs you two, and lock
him in his bedroom."

"It's going to be a long business," said Mr. Badger, sighing. "I've never seen Toad so determined."

And true enough, while he was locked in his room, Toad would arrange the bedroom chairs to look like a motor car.

Then he would pretend that he was in the driving seat and drive along – "poop-poop" until he had an accident.

One day, when Mole and Mr. Badger had gone out for a ramble in the woods, Rat went upstairs to see Toad and found him still in bed.

"Ratty," he murmured feebly, "would you go to the village quickly. And fetch a doctor. Even now it may be too late!"

Rat hurried from the room, being very careful, however, to lock the door behind him.

"It's best to be on the safe side," he said to himself.

"I'd better humour him and go," he thought. "If there's nothing really the matter, the doctor will tell him he's an old ass."

So he ran off to the village on his errand of mercy.

Little did he know that Toad had hopped out of bed as soon as he heard the key turn in the lock.

Toad got dressed quickly
in his best suit and filled his
pockets with money.

Then he took the sheets
off his bed. He tied them
together and fastened one
end to the centre mullion of
his window.

He scrambled out of the
window, held on to the
sheets very tightly, and slid
gently to the ground below.

Taking the opposite direction
to Rat, Toad scampered off
happily, whistling a merry tune.

Poor Rat felt a terrible fool when Mr. Badger and
Mole came back and he had to tell them that Toad
had escaped.

"You've been a bit of a duffer this time, Ratty," said
Mole. "Toad, too, of all animals!"

"He did it awfully well," said Rat.

Meanwhile, Toad, gay and irresponsible, walked briskly along.

"Smart piece of work that," he said to himself, chuckling.

And when he reached a little town, he went into the hotel and ordered a slap-up lunch for himself to celebrate his escape.

He was half-way through his meal when he heard a "poop-poop" and a motor car stopping outside.

The occupants came inside, and Toad could contain himself no longer. Out into the yard he went to have a look.

"I wonder if this sort of car *starts* easily," he murmured.

Of course, Toad just could not resist the temptation.

He got in, started the engine and drove out of the yard.

He drove out of the town and sped through the open country beyond.

He felt that he was Toad once more, Toad at his best, Toad the terror, the traffic-queller.

The miles were eaten up under him as he went. He knew not whither, living his hour, reckless of what might come to him…

"Let me see," said the Magistrate. "He is guilty of stealing a motor car, of driving dangerously and of cheeking the police. What's the stiffest penalty we can give him?"

"Twenty years," said the Clerk.
"Excellent!" said the Magistrate.

So poor Toad was taken off to prison, loaded with chains.

They had to drag him from the courthouse, shrieking and protesting; past the crowds in the market-place and across the drawbridge of the grim old castle.

They took the unhappy Toad past sentries and guardrooms full of grinning soldiers. They led him right to the door of the grimmest dungeon that lay in the heart of the innermost keep in the castle.

The rusty key creaked in the lock, the great door clanged behind him, and Toad was a helpless prisoner.

# Chapter 7

## THE PIPER AT THE GATES OF DAWN

Rat had been visiting Otter. When he came back, late one midsummer evening, he told Mole all about it while the pair of them sat in the cool on the river bank.

"The baby otter, Little Portly, is missing again," said Rat. "He's been missing for some days now and the otters have hunted everywhere for him."

"Otter told me that he's very anxious," Rat went on, "because Little Portly can't swim very well yet."

"Otter's going to spend the night watching by the ford – because that's where young Portly had his first swimming lesson and where he caught his first fish."

"So Otter goes there every night and watches – just on the off chance, you know."

Rat and Mole decided to get the boat out and paddle upstream.

"It's better than going to bed and doing *nothing*," said Mole.

They kept a good look-out for the baby otter and when the moon came up they could see much better.

They scanned the river from bank to bank, looking in the meadows and quiet gardens as they passed.

They searched all night long.
They landed on the bank to
explore the hedges, the hollow
trees, the ditches. Then they heard a
faint musical piping.

They went towards the sound
and it got louder and more distinct.

Suddenly they saw the piper, smiling at them, his pan-pipes in one hand.

And there was the baby otter, nestling between his hooves, sleeping soundly.

Then the sun rose, dazzling their eyes, and when they looked again, the vision of the piper had gone.

Little Portly woke up with a joyous squeak.

"Come along Rat," called Mole. "Think of poor Otter waiting anxiously up there by the ford."

So the two friends put the baby otter safely between them in the bottom of their boat and rowed up the river.

There, they were able to watch the joyous reunion between Otter and Little Portly.

## Chapter 8

# TOAD'S ADVENTURES

Chained up in his dungeon, all alone, Toad shed bitter tears and abandoned himself to despair.

"This is the end of everything," he wept. "How can I ever hope to be free again?"

And for several weeks he refused all the food brought to him by the grim and ancient gaoler.

But the gaoler had a daughter, a good-hearted girl who helped her father sometimes in the prison.

She was very fond of animals and she said to her father one day: "I can't bear to see poor Toad so unhappy and getting so thin."

"Let me look after him," she pleaded.

"Do what you like," said the gaoler.

So that very day, the gaoler's daughter went to see Toad, to talk to him and to tempt him with food.

At first he would not be comforted, but when she brought him tea and very thick hot buttered toast he started eating again.

And they had many interesting talks together.

She told him that she had an elderly aunt who was the washerwoman at the prison.

She suggested that, if Toad gave this lady a little money, she might be willing to let him have one of her dresses and an old bonnet so that he could escape from the castle.

And so, next morning, the girl brought her aunt to Toad's cell.

Shaking with laughter, the gaoler's daughter helped Toad to dress up in the cotton print gown, arranged the shawl and tied on the washerwoman's bonnet; all of which her aunt had brought in her bundle of washing.

Then the pair of them tied the old lady up to make it look as though the daring Toad had overpowered her to steal the clothes.

With quaking heart but firm
footstep, Toad made his way
through the castle.

The warders and the soldiers joked as they saw the
stout little figure in familiar clothes go walking by.

Every door and every gate was opened for him.

Even so, it seemed hours before he crossed the last
courtyard – and then he was walking across
the drawbridge.

Free!

Dizzy with the success of his daring exploit, Toad made his way to the railway station.

He went to the booking office to buy a ticket – and found to his horror that he had left all his money and belongings behind in the prison.

He pleaded with the booking-clerk, but he was pushed out of the way.

In despair again, he wandered down the platform to where the train was waiting. He told the engine driver all his troubles.

Luckily, the engine driver was a very kind man. He told the poor washerwoman that if she washed a few shirts for him she could have a lift in his cab.

Toad was very thrilled as the train sped along.

But after a while, the engine driver said they were being followed by another engine.

"And it's crowded with warders and policemen," he exclaimed.

So he slowed down enough for Toad to jump off as they passed through a thick wood.

He rolled down an embankment and scrambled into the wood. He watched his train get up speed again and disappear.

Then the pursuing engine roared past, everybody shouting, "Stop! Stop!"

Toad had a hearty laugh for the first time since he was thrown into prison.

Chapter 9

# THE FURTHER ADVENTURES OF TOAD

Toad slept that night in the hollow of a tree. He woke up next morning because his toes were cold.

But he soon forgot about that when he remembered that he was free!

He had all the world to himself that early summer morning and he strolled along the lanes until he came to a canal.

Round a bend in the canal came plodding a large horse, towing a barge. Steering the barge was a large, stout woman.

"A nice morning, Ma'am," she called to Toad as the barge drew level with him.

Toad replied politely and said that he was a poor washerwoman trying to get back to her home near Toad Hall.

"Toad Hall?" answered the barge-woman. "Why, I'm going that way."

"Toad's luck again!" thought Toad as he stepped lightly on board the barge. "I always come out on top."

But there was a surprise in store for Toad this time!

"You can get on with my washing for me," said the barge-woman.

Toad's back was aching and his wet paws were getting all crinkly.

The barge-woman suddenly laughed.

"Why, you can't wash at all," she said, and looked at him closely. "Well I never! A horrid, nasty Toad! And in my clean barge."

And she threw Toad over the side.

Toad hit the water with a splash and a splutter but he managed to swim to the steep bank and climb up.

He was very cross and looking for revenge.

Then he saw the horse which was towing the barge.

He ran after it, unfastened the tow-rope, jumped up on to the horse's back and went off at a gallop.

He had travelled a long way when he came to a
gipsy caravan where a man was sitting by a fire
of sticks.

From the pot which was hanging over the fire came
the most delicious smells.

Toad just sat there and sniffed hungrily.

"Want to sell that horse of yours?" asked the gipsy.

"Sell this beautiful horse?" exclaimed Toad. "Oh, no – it's out of the question."

But the gipsy continued to bargain with him and offered fifty pence.

Toad thought very carefully. He *was* very hungry and he had no money.

"Look here, gipsy," he said. "If you give me seventy-five pence, plus as much as I can possibly eat out of that pot, you shall have my horse."

So it was arranged and Toad stuffed and stuffed and kept asking for more.

After he had finished eating, Toad set off for the road once more, very pleased with himself.

He saw a car approaching and stood in the middle of the road to stop it.

But, oh dear! as it slowed down he recognised it as the car he had stolen.

Poor Toad collapsed in despair in the road.

Toad thought that the people in the car would send for the police.

But, no. All they saw was a poor old washerwoman lying in the road, and they decided to take her to the nearest village.

So they lifted Toad into the car and as they moved off his courage began to revive.

And when they had gone a little way, he asked if he could drive the car!

How they laughed! "Let the old lady try!"

Toad eagerly took the wheel and drove off, very slowly at first, then faster and faster.

And when he started boasting what a clever Toad he was, they realised their mistake and tried to grab him.

The car went through a hedge and they all landed in a muddy pool.

## Chapter 10

## 'LIKE SUMMER TEMPEST

## CAME HIS TEARS'

Toad ran off as fast as he could go, chased by the men from the car.

He was looking back over his shoulder when – SPLASH – he ran straight into the river!

Breathless and spluttering, he floated along a little way with the stream and presently he saw a big dark hole in the river bank.

It was Rat's house – and Rat was there to rescue him.

As soon as Toad was indoors, he started boasting to Rat about his adventures.

"Toad," said Rat gravely, "You go upstairs and take off that old cotton rag and put on some of my clothes.

Now stop swaggering and arguing! I'll have something to say to you later."

Toad washed and
changed his clothes
and stood looking
at himself in the
mirror with pride
and pleasure.

Feeling much better, he went downstairs and ate a
large lunch prepared by Rat. When they had both
finished eating, Rat told him how the Stoats and the
Weasels had taken over Toad Hall.

While Toad was away, Rat explained, Badger and Mole had gone to stay at Toad Hall to keep it aired.

Then one dark night, bands of weasels, stoats and ferrets had attacked the house and driven Mole and Badger out into the cold.

"I'll jolly well soon see about that!" said Toad,
grabbing a stick and marching rapidly down the road
to Toad Hall.

But when he got to the front gate, a yellow ferret
with a gun suddenly popped out and fired at Toad.

BANG! And a bullet whistled over his head.

But Toad was not going to give in.

He went back to Rat's house.

He got out the boat.

And he rowed up the river towards Toad Hall. All seemed peaceful and quiet until – CRASH! – a great stone, thrown from the bridge, smashed through the bottom of the boat and it sank!

Toad struggled back to tell Rat all about it. And Rat
prepared a big supper for him.

Just as they finished, there was a knock at the door –
and there was Mr. Badger.

He solemnly shook Toad by the paw.

"This is a poor homecoming," he said.
"Unhappy Toad."

A little while later, Mole arrived too and they talked about the situation.

Badger said, "The stoats are on guard at every point. It's quite useless to think of attacking the place. They're too strong for us."

"Then it's all over," sobbed Toad. "I shall never see my dear Toad Hall any more…"

"Cheer up, Toady," cried Badger encouragingly. "I'm going to tell you a secret. There is an underground passage from the river bank that leads right into the middle of Toad Hall – and there's a banquet there tomorrow night."

"We shall creep out quietly…" cried Mole.

"With pistols and swords…" shouted Rat.

"And whack 'em and whack 'em," cried Toad in ecstasy.

Next morning, Toad slept till late. When he did
come down to breakfast, he found that Rat was
collecting swords and pistols.

The Badger said that all they would need was sticks,
once they got into Toad Hall.

"It's as well to be on the safe side," said Rat.

Then Mole came in.

He told them that he had been up to Toad Hall dressed in the old washer-woman's dress. He had spoken to the guards and told them that all the animals were going to attack Toad Hall from the *outside*.

"Oh, you silly ass, Mole!" cried Toad. "You've been and spoilt everything!"

But Badger could see the sense in what Mole had done. "Good Mole!" he said approvingly.

This made Toad a bit jealous, especially because he could not make out what it was that Mole had done that was so clever.

So Mole took him outside, and made Toad tell him about all his adventures from beginning to end.

## Chapter 11

# THE RETURN OF ULYSSES

When it began to grow dark, they all assembled in Rat's parlour, and Rat gave each one his sword and pistols.

But Badger just laughed good-humouredly.

"I'm going to do all I've got to do with this here stick," he said.

When they were ready, Badger took a lantern and led them along by the river and then into a hole in the river bank.

Mole and Rat followed silently, but when it came to Toad's turn, of course he managed to slip and fell into the water.

He was hauled out by his friends, but Badger was very cross.

A little while later, they were creeping along the secret passage, which was dark and cold and damp.

Toad was hurrying to keep up with the others when he bumped into Rat, who bumped into Mole, who fell over.

Badger thought they were being attacked from behind and he very nearly shot Toad with his pistol.

After that, Rat kept a firm grip on Toad's shoulder to keep him out of trouble. And so they groped and shuffled along the secret passage until they came to a trap door.

Badger said, "Now, boys, all together!"

They found themselves in the pantry with only a door between them and the banqueting hall.

They could hear the Weasels cheering and singing.
Badger cried, "Follow me!" and he flung the door
open wide.

My!
What a squealing and a
squeaking and a screeching
filled the air!

Mole had gone outside to deal with the sentries.

"It's all over," he reported back. "They had been expecting an attack from outside, but as soon as they heard the shrieks and yells inside the hall, they threw down their rifles and fled."

"They've all disappeared by now, and I've got their rifles."

And so the four friends sat down to a great supper of chicken and jelly and trifle.

Next day, Badger told Toad that he must hold a banquet to celebrate, and that he should write the invitations himself.

While the others were out, Toad did as he was told, but he also included a programme for the banquet. This was to be full of boastful speeches and songs by Toad all about Toad.

He gave the letters to one of the weasels to post.

When Badger, Rat and Mole came
back, they eyed Toad with a good deal
of suspicion. They had met the weasel
carrying Toad's invitations and had
taken them all off him.

"No speeches and no songs," said
Rat firmly. "You know you must
turn over a new leaf – and now is the
time to begin!"

Toad thought for a long while.
Eventually he said, "All right – I
won't boast any more."

"From now on, I will be a very different Toad. You will never have to blush for me again."

"But oh dear, oh dear, this is a hard world!"

Toad went up to his bedroom. At first he was very sad.

Then he began to smile.

Then he giggled.

He locked the door, drew the curtains, arranged all the chairs in a semi-circle and sang his boastful song very loudly to the empty chairs.

After that he felt better.

At last the hour for the banquet began to draw near and while Toad was still making a speech to his empty bedroom, the first of the animals began to arrive.

They were all dressed up in best suits.

Upstairs, Toad finished off his speech with a flourish and a bow to the vacant chairs.

Then he heaved a deep sigh; a long, long, long sigh.

Then he straightened his bow tie, adjusted his jacket, then put a gracefully modest expression on his face.

He went downstairs to welcome all the guests to the banquet. The animals cheered when he entered and congratulated him.

But Toad only smiled faintly and murmured, "Not at all."

He was indeed an altered Toad.

After all this excitement, the four animals continued to be friends. They would often take a stroll together in the Wild Wood and it was pleasing to see how the mother weasels would bring out their young ones and point them out.

"There goes the great Mr. Toad, and the gallant Water Rat, and the famous Mr. Mole," they would say.

And, when their children were naughty, they would tell them that the terrible grey Badger would come and get them if they didn't behave themselves. Which was a little unfair on Badger because he was rather fond of children.

But it never failed!